Rifka
Sings

ISBN: 978-1-936208-60-9

Illustrations: Josephine Beachy
Cover design and layout: Felicia Kern

Printed November 2011
Printed in the USA

Published by:
TGS International
P.O. Box 355 · Berlin, Ohio 44610 USA
Phone: 330-893-4828
Fax: 330-893-2305
www.tgsinternational.com

TGS000421

Rifka Sings

Harvey Yoder

Table of Contents

Rifka From Sudan

CHAPTER ONE

"Swing, swing, swing!" eight-year-old Rifka sang as she kicked her right foot against the ground to keep herself moving. The shade from the limbs of the tree above her only slightly cooled the very warm air of Sudan, the largest country in Africa.

"Swing, swing, swing," Rifka chanted again as she sailed back and forth on the rope swing, enjoying the breeze as she pumped herself to greater heights.

"Mamma is sleeping, Daddy is working, Rifka is swinging." Rifka sang to herself, making up her own song.

Rifka loved to sing. She loved to sing almost as well as she enjoyed swinging. Because she was the youngest child, born seven years after Mahmoud, her closest sibling, Rifka was raised almost as an only child. Her brother was away in a boarding school, and the other seven children appeared only on weekends. Several of them were already married with families of their own.

From the tree above, a flock of parakeets chattered and scolded, their bright yellow and orange wings flitting about like tropical flowers let loose in the breeze.

"Samboni, come swing with me!" Rifka called to their faithful watchdog, but there was no response from the big black dog snoozing beside the house. Posted there, he could keep a watchful eye on the front gate that led to the street. A high metal fence hid their home from the view of traffic and passersby, but Samboni always heard when someone rattled the latch on the front gate. Even though it looked as though he was sleeping, he would instantly spring up if someone stopped by, barking to let Rifka's family know they had visitors.

When the prayer call sounded from the mosque, Rifka knew it was three o'clock. The call came loudly from a tall minaret, the tower that soared above the Muslim place of worship.

Five times a day the prayer call came. It reminded all the followers of Muhammad to stop whatever they were doing and kneel in prayer. They knelt with their faces toward Mecca, a city in Saudi Arabia, which they considered the holiest city in the world.

Rifka watched the back door to see if her mother would call her inside to pray. If Mamma was sleeping, she might not wake up and call her inside, but if she was awake, she would surely come and call her.

"Rifka!"

Mamma was awake. "Coming," Rifka answered, sliding off the swing and running inside. She kicked off her sandals and ran to wash her feet and arms.

Her mother's dark face was beaded with sweat, but her curly black hair, streaked with gray, was brushed smoothly back from her face. She was dressed in a loose, cool gown called a *tob (tōb)*, a garment that most Arab Sudanese women wore inside the house.

Rifka herself was wearing a short, loose dress. Only after she became a teenager would she also wear a *tob*.

Rifka followed her mother into a small room off the main room of the house. There, she stood beside her mother, facing her prayer mat, and began to recite the afternoon prayers.

"In the name of Allah, the most compassionate, the most merciful, we offer all praise to you. To you alone we bring our worship. Show us the straight path. Forgive our wrongs. Your anger is against those who do not follow you. There is none like you."

Ever since she could remember, Rifka had said the same prayers every day. The words melted together into phrases that had a song-like quality, and Rifka enjoyed the chant. Though she did not really know what the words meant, Rifka didn't mind. Something about their familiarity was soothing and calming.

As she recited the prayers, Rifka knelt down and touched her forehead on the prayer mat. Her mother didn't kneel because she said her knees were getting too stiff. She said Allah would understand.

Rifka knew her father and many of the men in their city of Khartoum, the capital city of Sudan, were in the mosque right now, also saying the same prayers. Rifka had occasionally gone to the mosque with her mother on special days of worship.

Her prayers finished, Rifka stood up. She and her mother left the small room, and Rifka sniffed hungrily.

"I want to eat outside," Rifka begged when they entered the dining room. The teapot was already waiting alongside a plate of cookies.

"Sit here with me," her mother told her, shaking her head slightly. "It is too hot outside."

"I don't mind," Rifka pouted. "I like the heat."

Rifka's mother looked at her active daughter, at the brown face and sparkling black eyes now half hidden in a scowl. "I don't know how you can like the heat. Even though it is warm in here, it is not nearly as hot as outside."

"May I?" Rifka begged after her mother had poured the tea into a mug. She took two small cookies and nibbled on them.

Her mother waved her hand in dismissal. "All right," she said wearily. "I am too old to have a young daughter like you. Here I am, almost fifty years old, and I have a young girl to look after."

Rifka did not stay to listen to her mother's sighs. Instead, she took several more cookies, slipped into her sandals, and went back outside.

Samboni eyed the young girl hopefully, and sure enough, as Rifka went past the dog, she tossed part of a cookie to him. He expertly caught it with a snap of his head.

Rifka was used to being careful with the hot tea while she walked. She held her right arm out to keep the hot liquid from spilling on her.

The swing was waiting for her, and she sat down carefully. Then she began sipping her hot tea. The sun shone still hotter as the long day wore on, and the leaves on the tree overhead hung limp as the sun beat down unmercifully.

It was a normal day for young Rifka. Her life had hardly changed since she could remember, except when she had started attending public school down the street when she was six years old. There, five days a week, Rifka attended school with the other children from their part of the city. She had learned to read and write and figure. She had even studied a foreign language, English. The teacher said it might be useful to know someday.

The students' school uniforms made it difficult to tell

which of them came from poor families and which ones came from wealthy homes. But Rifka knew that many of her classmates came from much poorer families than she did. "My daddy works for the government," Rifka told her classmates more than once. "He has a good job," she would say as she ate her snack in front of the others' watching eyes during the midmorning break. Occasionally she would share something with her best friend, Taj.

She didn't know exactly what her father did in the place called the Ministry of the Interior, but she knew it was important.

Her father never talked about his job at home. In fact, whenever he came home from the office, he would collapse into a soft chair and hardly move except to turn the pages of the newspapers he was always reading. Nevertheless, Rifka knew his job was important, and it made her feel good to be the daughter of such an important man.

Soon after five o'clock, Samboni rose quickly to his feet, wagging his tail as he hurried to the front gate. Rifka wondered if her father had come home.

Yes, there was his familiar figure opening the gate. As always, his hair was wrapped in a white turban, and a long white robe reached below his knees, covering his thin white trousers. The tired man ignored his daughter and entered the house. Rifka kept on swinging and making up her own song.

The day is ending soon,
And then we will eat our dinner, mamma and I,
While father eats in his chair.
Then, when the dark comes and covers the city
And the stars are switched on,
Then, then, then, will I go to bed.
Samboni watches over us and we sleep;
We sleep and we sleep until the next morning.

Rifka pushed her feet firmly against the ground and soared up among the tree branches.

Then tomorrow we get up and after tea,
I go to school, to school, to school.
All morning, all morning, I am at school,
And then at noon, I come home—

Home to swing, to swing,
To wait for the next day, and then
I do it all over again, again, and again,
This is my life in Sudan, my country.

Rifka loved making up songs. As she heard her own voice telling the story of her life, it made her feel important.

Swing, swing, swing!
I swing, swing, swing!

The shadows began to cover the yard as the African sun slid toward the horizon, yet Rifka kept on swinging and singing. Swinging and singing. Singing and swinging.

Moving Away?

CHAPTER TWO

Samboni stood up and wagged his tail as Rifka unlocked the front gate. Slipping inside, she carefully closed the gate and locked it again. School had been uneventful. Rifka was ready for her lunch.

She rounded the corner of the house to enter through the back door when she heard voices inside.

She stopped short. Her father was home in the middle of a school day! She recognized his voice, talking to her mother.

For her father to be home in the middle of the day was as unusual as if the sun had suddenly stopped in its slow journey across the African sky. Day after day, their lives marched on in regular patterns, predictable and orderly. Now, something was not quite right.

Opening the door, Rifka stepped inside. Her parents were standing in the main room facing each other. They ignored their daughter's puzzled gaze.

"I have been selected as the senior officer in the Ministry of the Interior to represent Sudan in England. This is important for our country," Father said. "For a long time, Sudan has not been properly represented in other countries. Now we will take our place among the nations with pride. *Allahu akbar (ä lä ' hu äk' bär)!*"[1]

"To live in a foreign country will not be easy, Muhammad!" Mamma's voice was sharp.

Rifka knew this was something serious. Mamma used Father's name, Muhammad, only when something extraordinary was happening. Like when she had found out that someone had entered their house while they were gone. Or when she realized that the thieves had stolen a lot of money.

"Our government will pay for everything," Father explained. "We will have a fine apartment with many rooms."

---

[1] *Allahu akbar* is an Arabic expression that means *Allah is the greatest.*

"A maid then," Mamma decided.

"Oh, yes," Father answered, sounding relieved. He seemed happy that Mamma had not said no.

Mamma sat down. "It is all coming so suddenly," she said, fanning herself. "Two weeks is not a long time."

Then, for the first time, she noticed Rifka. Fine lines appeared on her forehead. "What will we do with our daughter? Do we need to put her in a boarding school?"

Father turned his dark eyes toward his daughter also. "Hmm," he said thoughtfully, "we will have to consider the matter."

Rifka did not ask more about what was happening. She did not say anything. She had been taught not to speak unless spoken to, and she had learned that if she waited long enough, her questions would often be answered. So, she waited.

"Oh, so many decisions," Mamma suddenly moaned. "This is not easy." She looked long and hard at Father.

Rifka felt the room whirl around her as the impact of the words "boarding school" suddenly hit her. *Go live away from home in a place full of strangers?* She knew some of the girls at her school had at one time attended boarding schools. She had gotten a distinct feeling that they did not enjoy their time there.

"I will inquire about the prospects of her attending school in England," Father decided. "It may be an advantage for her to be educated in a country where English is spoken. Yes, I will inquire."

The hollow space inside Rifka that was always ready for lunch suddenly churned. Today, instead of heading to the kitchen where her lunch was waiting for her, she turned and dashed outside. Her head was spinning as she tried to absorb what she had just heard. She sat on the swing and stared at the school uniform she had forgotten to change.

Represent Sudan in England. The phrase kept repeating itself in Rifka's mind. She knew what "represent" meant. In school she had learned how sometimes officials were called to live in other countries in order to promote their own countries' interests.

So Father has been asked to represent Sudan. That must be an honor!

Rifka searched her mind, trying to remember her geography lessons. *Where exactly is England?* She had a faint recollection of a small, rather oddly shaped island off the continent of Europe with the word "England" written on it.

Father and Mamma are going to move to England without me? Rifka felt her stomach lurch again. *And send me to a boarding school?*

"Rifka, come eat your lunch," Mamma's voice came from the open door.

Rifka wanted to tell her mother she was not hungry. She wanted to say her stomach was in rebellion at the idea of food.

But she said nothing except her normal, "Yes, Mamma," the way she had been taught to respond.

"Rifka, change your clothes," Mamma said, frowning slightly as she saw that her daughter was still wearing her school uniform.

"Yes, Mamma," Rifka said again, her eyes on the tile floor beneath her feet.

She went to her bedroom and put on her everyday dress. Then she went to the kitchen and sat on the stool, looking at the plate of food in front of her. Taking small bites of the seasoned chickpeas, she chewed each mouthful a long time before forcing herself to swallow. More than once she felt sure the food wasn't going to stay in her stomach, but somehow Rifka managed to keep each bite down.

She could hear her mother moving around in the next room, rummaging through drawers. Every once in a while Rifka could hear an exasperated sigh coming through the open doors. "So much to do in just two weeks' time," her mother moaned more than once.

Father must have returned to the office after his midday visit, Rifka realized, for she could not hear him moving around anywhere.

When the mound of food was finally gone, Rifka went back outside and sat down on the swing. But the turmoil in her stomach would not let her swing. Instead, she sat motionless as her mind spun in dizzying circles.

The heat continued to build, and Rifka felt small rivulets of moisture run down her back under her dress. She wanted to swing back and forth to cool off, but she couldn't move. The heavy weight inside kept her motionless.

Finally she slid off the swing and slipped through the

back door. Inside, the air was cooler.

There was only silence inside. Mamma was probably taking her afternoon nap. Rifka went to her own room and sat on her narrow bed. She stared at the white walls. She looked at the blue and yellow curtain covering the window and keeping some of the heat outside. Then she lay down, curling her legs up against her stomach and closing her eyes. Little sparkles of light swam against her closed eyelids. Rifka clenched her hands tightly together and lay very still.

Rifka sat bolt upright. At first, everything seemed normal, just like any other day when she woke from a nap. Suddenly, though, she remembered the events of the day, and once more she felt the tightness in her stomach. She could hear her parents talking again. Father must have returned from the office.

"We will take Rifka with us," Father's voice rang out loudly. "I inquired and we can enroll her in a school in England for no charge. She will receive an excellent

education! She will learn to speak English fluently. That will be a valuable part of her education."

"Why does she need to learn a foreign language?" Mamma asked. "Sudanese girls don't need to learn English. Rifka will marry like her sisters and have a family."

"Oh, times are changing," Father said. "Now girls are getting jobs in offices and making careers for themselves. Even her chances of getting a good husband will increase if she is educated."

"I never learned to read and write," Mamma said swiftly. "I have managed."

"Of course you have," Father said. "But like I said, some things are changing, even here in Sudan. Where is Rifka?"

"Here I am, Father," Rifka replied, appearing in the main room.

"You will be going with us to England," Father told his daughter, a thin smile spreading over his face. "You will go to school there and get a good education. What do you think about that?"

Rifka stared up at her father. At first, she just nodded. Then she managed to say, "Yes, Father, a good education." She nodded again.

She wanted to say more but couldn't. She wanted to tell her father how happy she was that she could stay with her parents instead of being shipped off to a boarding school. She wanted to tell him that it was scary to think of moving to a different country, but not nearly as scary as thinking she might be left behind.

Instead, she asked quietly, "Where is England, Father?"

Her father took her into his office and pulled out an atlas. He pointed to the island that Rifka had seen in her mind and said, "Right there. See, here is Sudan and there is England, where we will live very soon. We will fly there in an airplane, and I will go to work and you will go to school. We will have a fine place to live, and Mamma will have a maid."

Rifka could hear that her father was excited about the coming move, and a little of his excitement spilled over to her. "Yes, Father," she replied, and for some reason the funny feeling in her stomach went away. The world stopped spinning in dizzying circles, and suddenly Rifka realized she was hungry.

London
CHAPTER THREE

Rifka stared out the airplane window to the ground below. A misty rain covered the runway with moisture. Outside the airplane, water dripped off the yellow hats of busy workers dressed in matching yellow raincoats.

The intercom crackled as the flight attendant gave final instructions to the passengers. Then the plane came to a stop, and there was a rush of activity as people stood up. They began opening the overhead compartments and taking out their belongings.

Beside her, Rifka's mother pulled her veil even closer around her face and sighed again. Rifka could see the worry in her eyes.

The flight from Sudan had begun only that morning. Even though it had been a scary experience at first, Rifka had enjoyed the adventure.

"I will get our bags," Father told them. He had been sitting beside the aisle, and now he got up and reached for their carry-on luggage.

Rifka unlatched her seatbelt. She pulled her blue backpack toward her and lifted it onto her lap.

The long line of passengers began moving toward the front of the airplane. Father joined the line, and Rifka and Mamma fell in step behind him.

Rifka clutched her backpack, thankful that she was sandwiched between her parents. As she headed toward the door of the plane, she saw the friendly faces of the flight attendants. She smiled shyly and looked away.

Then they were inside the airport. The high ceiling towered above them, and the sounds of hundreds of footsteps echoed on the tile floors of the wide halls.

Rifka had studied hard in English class back in Khartoum. But now she realized that her English was really not very good. It had not been good enough to understand the instructions that had been announced over the intercom on their flight. It was not good enough to understand most of the signs that filled the airport.

Rifka followed her parents as they moved with the crowd toward the exit. There they stood in line as officials checked passports.

There were businessmen in suits, teenagers in casual clothes, and young ladies sporting the latest fashions. Rifka could not stop staring at the diverse crowd. There were people in a variety of brown and black skin tones, but they were far outnumbered by those with white skin. Rifka had never seen this many white-skinned people in her entire life. She stared in wonder. A young girl in front of her had a ponytail of light blond hair that swung back and forth. Rifka wondered how it could be real. Her own hair was dark and curly. She thought how easy it must be for the girl to brush out the mane of hair. Rifka wanted to reach out and touch it, but she didn't dare.

They had come to a desk. An officer looked at them through a glass partition. He asked Rifka's father a few questions and stamped their passports one by one. They were through.

Next they went to get their checked-in luggage. They stood among other passengers and waited until their suitcases finally came out on the moving belt.

Rifka felt bewildered by the bustling activity of the airport. She shivered inside her jacket and wondered at the cold. Finally, a man who seemed to recognize Father met them, and they went outside. "Welcome," the man said in Arabic, and Rifka was so glad to hear her own language.

Outside, the cold dampness set her teeth to chattering, and she hugged her backpack tightly, trying to warm herself.

"This is terrible!" Mamma moaned as they walked across white lines painted on the street and entered a huge building where cars were parked on each level. "How can it be this cold?"

Father did not hear Mamma because he walked ahead, beside their escort. As usual in Sudanese culture, the women followed the men. Rifka shivered all over as the damp air seeped through her thin clothes and penetrated to her bones.

It was warmer in the car, but by now Rifka was so cold

she could not keep her teeth from chattering.

"Here we are," their escort told them a few minutes later as he pulled into a narrow driveway and stopped the car.

Rifka looked out the car window at a gray stone building four stories high. Numerous sets of steps led to identical doors. Each door was flanked by small windows and shadowed by a small protruding balcony above it.

They entered the building and started up an inner staircase. After going up three flights of stairs, the man unlocked a door and led them into their apartment.

Mamma sank down on a chair and shivered. "It is so cold in here," she said in a weak voice.

"The English do not heat their houses well," their host told them nervously. He turned to Father, "You will probably want to go shopping soon. You will need thicker clothes."

Rifka felt that even if she wore all the clothes she owned, she would still not be warm. She huddled on a soft sofa.

"There are blankets in here somewhere," their escort said, and disappeared into a room. He came back and

placed two blankets respectfully on the sofa beside Rifka. Rifka passed one to Mamma's eager hands and wrapped herself in the other one. Father followed the man as he showed him the apartment.

A friend of their host soon brought lunch, and they all sat down around a tiny table in the kitchen. The kitchen was hardly bigger than their hallway at home, but Rifka didn't spend much time thinking about that. Instead, she gratefully drank hot tea. She savored every swallow as the delicious warmth slid down her throat.

The rest of the day was spent settling in. Helping Mamma unpack suitcases took Rifka's mind off the penetrating cold. Father had gone to see the building where he would be working.

Sometime in the afternoon there was a knock at the door. Mamma opened it timidly. It was the promised maid, Shaima. Finally, Mamma had someone to talk to. She was able to ask the maid all kinds of questions, because Shaima spoke Arabic. Shaima showed Mamma how to turn up the heat, although she warned them it would never warm up enough to keep them as warm as they had been in Sudan.

Rifka liked the cheery yellow room that was going to be her bedroom. It was very tiny, barely big enough to hold the narrow bed. There was no window at all, but an overhead ceiling light made it bright, and a small white lamp beside her bed made a circle of yellow on the rug below.

Everything in the apartment felt crowded and cramped. Only the living room was spacious and furnished with ample seating. In the bathroom, the sink was squished into a corner. There was no bathtub, only a shower. Mamma shook her head when she saw the arrangement. "Oh, why did we ever come here?" she sighed.

In the living room, two large windows on one wall let some light into the room. Rifka walked to the windows and pushed away the white lace curtains that covered them. She looked across the narrow street to another building that looked almost identical to their own. Below one window, someone had planted red flowers in a box. They made a pleasant spot of color on the drab gray walls.

That evening, Father returned and they ate the meal that Shaima prepared for them. Then there was nothing else to do, so Rifka shivered through her shower and eagerly crawled under the covers of her bed. Her teeth chattered as she curled up, hugging her knees against her. The apartment might have been a little warmer than it had been when they first arrived, but the shivering family could not feel the difference.

Outside on the street, cars continued to rush past, echoing in the narrow canyon between the apartment buildings.

Rifka felt bewildered by the rapid changes that had come into her life. She thought back to the home they had left just that morning. She thought about her swing underneath the huge shade tree in her yard. She thought about the songs she used to sing and about the hours she had spent there under the warm Sudanese sun.

But now, the warmth was gone and there was no sun. She missed the huge tree with her swing. That tree had been a comforting canopy. Rifka wondered if England even had any trees. She did not remember seeing any in their journey from the airport. Just buildings and cars and people and buses and taxis.

A tear trickled down Rifka's cheek. She did not like this country. She did not like this tiny, cramped apartment they were supposed to live in. The thought of what lay ahead of her made Rifka's stomach want to churn. School! She was sure she would not like it either.

School
CHAPTER FOUR

"We welcome Rifka to our school," the teacher said as she faced the class, her hand resting gently on the newcomer's shoulder. "She is from Sudan. Make her feel welcome."

"Welcome to our school, Rifka!" the children chorused.

Rifka did not see the many smiling faces turned toward her. She did not see the curious eyes of the pupils as they gazed at her brown skin, black eyes, and black hair. Remembering how her parents had taught her to behave in public, Rifka kept her eyes on the floor and did not smile.

The teacher showed her where her desk was and Rifka

sat down, arranging her brown skirt under the desk. Her school uniform matched the other students' outfits exactly. When her father had registered her for school, he had been given the address of the store where they could buy the required uniforms. Shaima had taken Rifka to the store and helped her select a yellow blouse and a brown skirt and jacket, just her size. They bought three sets of uniforms, several pairs of long stockings, and a pair of shoes.

During this shopping trip, Rifka had been amazed at the variety of items available to purchase. But even more amazing was how easily Shaima switched from Arabic when speaking to Rifka and to English when speaking to the salesclerks. How was it possible to talk so fluently in more than one language?

Now, sitting at her desk in school, Rifka listened closely to the English conversation around her. Thankfully, the teacher, Miss Harbon, spoke slowly and distinctly whenever she addressed Rifka. But even when she did not understand what her teacher was saying, Rifka nodded her head. It would be impolite to show Miss Harbon she did not understand. In Sudan, that was considered an insult.

Class began with arithmetic, and when the papers were placed on her desk, Rifka was relieved to see familiar number problems, all of them quite manageable. It was the four reading problems at the end of the lesson, however, that stumped her.

Straining to use her limited English, she tried to sound out the words. The boy in the problem was named Bob, but she could not understand what he was doing or what she was supposed to figure out. She recognized the word "shop," but the string of hard words after that made no sense at all.

"Let me read it for you," Miss Harbon said kindly. She read slowly and distinctly. Then she asked, "Do you understand?"

Rifka heard the inflection in her teacher's voice, so she nodded. Miss Harbon moved on.

Rifka tried again. This time it made more sense. Bob went to a shop to buy some things Rifka had never heard of. Even when she sounded out the words "mitt" and "bat," they made no sense to her. But, she decided, if he went to a shop, he probably needed to find out how much the things cost, so she added the numbers behind the items together and put the sum on her paper.

Once more, Miss Harbon was beside her. She saw that Rifka had put an answer down and said, “Good work, Rifka. Now, if he gives five pounds, how much money will he get back?”

Rifka looked at the problem again. *Oh, yes. That is what “change” means. Not as in changing clothes.* She wrote the numbers down and subtracted.

“Very good,” Miss Harbon said as she watched.

“Marguerite, will you read the next problem for Rifka? I’m sure she will soon be able to understand the problems herself, but for right now, we will help her.”

The girl who came over from the next desk had light brown, bouncy hair. Marguerite smiled at Rifka and read the problem to her. “Do you understand?”

Even though she didn’t, Rifka nodded her head. She could not be rude to this girl by letting her know she did not understand her.

“Okay,” Marguerite said cheerfully and went back to her desk.

Rifka read the problem for herself. Thankfully, hearing

12
4
+5

Marguerite pronounce the words out loud helped her understand a few of them, and she guessed at the meaning of the rest.

The third reading problem was easier, and Rifka actually understood it. But she couldn't understand the last one, so she looked shyly at her new friend. Thankfully, Marguerite came to her rescue.

A bell rang, and the pupils all rose to their feet. Marguerite smiled encouragingly at Rifka and whispered, "Gym." This meant nothing to Rifka, but she fell in line and followed the others down the hall and into a large exercise room. She joined them in a bewildering maze of movements: bending, hopping, and marching around in circles.

The gym teacher was a slender lady who energetically led the girls in their exercises. Rifka tried to follow the example of the others and often failed miserably, but everyone was helpful and did not seem to mind.

Afterward there were more classes, and Rifka's head began to ache as she vainly tried to understand what was happening. More than once, Marguerite had to help her, and sometimes another girl, Barbara, also helped her.

At midday they went to the cafeteria for lunch. “No pork for my daughter,” her father had told Mrs. Smelcher when he had registered Rifka. The principal had nodded and said, “We understand. There are other Muslim children in our school.”

As they pushed their trays along in front of the cafeteria bar, the students were served by the kitchen staff standing behind the bar. “Pork?” a middle-aged woman asked, looking at Rifka, her spoon suspended in midair.

Rifka did not say anything because she didn’t know she was being addressed.

“I say, do you want pork, or are you one of those Muslims?” This time the lady spoke louder.

“Yes, she is a Muslim,” Marguerite said. “She doesn’t want pork.”

The woman shrugged and dumped some vegetables on Rifka’s plate. But Rifka had a hard time eating anything, because as she sat alone in the crowded cafeteria, she felt a familiar weight in her stomach.

The afternoon was worse. The textbooks were very hard to understand, and the weight in her stomach felt even heavier. The damp cold bored deep inside her, and she worked hard to keep from shivering visibly. More than once she had to fight away the tears that threatened to spill down her cheeks. She longed for the end of the school day to arrive. If it had not been for the kindness of Miss Harbon and Marguerite, Rifka would have felt even worse.

"Choir practice," Miss Harbon said, rising to her feet.

Rifka had no idea what that meant, but once more she followed the others down the hall. They entered the gymnasium again, but instead of assembling on the floor, the students stood in a group, facing their teacher.

"Let's see," Miss Harbon said, taking Rifka by the shoulder. "We'll put you right next to Barbara. You will be able to follow her strong soprano."

When the first notes of the piano sounded melodiously in the huge room, Rifka looked at the booklet Barbara shared with her. Were they going to sing?

Something stirred in Rifka's heart. Back in Sudan—which now seemed so far away—Rifka had always loved to sing the Arabic folk songs. Would she know the songs they were singing here?

The students sang four songs. None of them sounded

like the songs Rifka knew. She was amazed at how different the singing sounded. The pupils' voices rose and fell in regular patterns, their voices blending together beautifully as Miss Harbon directed. Occasionally the teacher would stop and give direction and encouragement to those who struggled to keep up with the rest.

Suddenly the day was over! Right after choir practice a bell rang, and Marguerite said with a wave, "Goodbye, see you in the morning." Rifka made her way to the sidewalk and headed for the apartment.

That night as she lay in bed, her mind replayed the day. School had been such a bewildering series of events. The English words swam in her mind, and the faces of Miss Harbon and Marguerite and Barbara flashed in front of her closed eyes and vanished again.

The melody of a song from choir practice surfaced in her mind. Rifka hummed snatches of it softly to herself. When it ended, she tried again. This time, she remembered more of the tune. Once more, she hummed the easy melody.

Some words came seemingly out of nowhere. "Jesus . . . joy of loving hearts . . . fount of life . . . light of men."

Rifka hummed in place of the words she had forgotten.

Over and over she sang what she could, trying to remember all the words. "Joy" and "light" and "men" she knew, but who was Jesus? She had never heard that word before. In spite of the strain of the harrowing day, it was good to sing again. It was the first time she had sung since they arrived in London one week ago.

Then she fell asleep and dreamed about white-skinned girls and arithmetic problems. She dreamed about exercises in the gym and vegetables in the cafeteria. Throughout the dream, the melody of a song floated up and down, in and around her dreams. "Jesus . . . joy of loving hearts . . ."

Outside, the noise of the big city of London continued unabated, taxi horns blaring, brakes screeching, and the sirens of emergency vehicles blasting as the drivers raced to scenes of accidents. But Rifka continued to sleep and dream, the pleasant melody of the new song echoing in her mind.

Singing Once More

CHAPTER FIVE

"Good morning!" Rifka said cheerfully, running up the steps to the school.

"Rifka! How are you?" Marguerite and Barbara and several of their classmates greeted her.

"I am now good," Rifka said with a bounce. "I have now been in school for 'tree,' no, three months."

"You are so different than when you first came," Marguerite said. "You talk!"

The girls laughed together. Rifka nodded. "Now I know to talk the English!" she laughed.

The warning bell rang, and the girls turned and entered the building. Even the weather had warmed up a little, and Rifka had learned it did not always rain in London. However, she still dressed very warmly. The cold and damp never quite seemed to go away, even though it was April.

"Good morning!" Miss Harbon said as the girls entered the classroom. She went to the window and looked out. "The sun! It is so good to see sunshine again! I have lived in England all my life, and I can never get enough sunshine." She opened her arms wide and closed her eyes, basking in the warm rays.

The girls laughed and crowded beside their teacher, imitating her. "The sun! Oh, the sun! I love the sun!" Rifka improvised words to fit a tune they had been learning in choir practice.

The other girls joined in, and their voices rose in volume.

"The sun! Oh, the sun!" Rifka sang, and the rest of the class echoed her words.

"I love the sun! I love the sun!"

Miss Harbon sang out a new phrase.

"Oh, Lord, we thank you! Thank you for the sun!"

The girls repeated her words as she continued.

"You are worthy of our praise! We thank you, Lord!"

Several of the girls began humming softly as Miss Harbon sang the words. The music swelled in the classroom.

Miss Harbon continued to sing.

We bring you praise!
We bring you glory!
Thank you for the sunshine!
Thank you for the rain!

Just then a cloud covered the sun, and the familiar chill settled into the room.

"Oh, Miss Harbon! You said 'Thank you for the rain,' and the sun went away!" Barbara said quickly.

"So I did," Miss Harbon agreed. Then she burst into song again.

We bring you praise!
We bring you glory!
Thank you for the sunshine of Jesus!
The sunshine of our hearts!

As if on cue, the sun broke through the clouds once more. The girls clapped and laughed with joy.

"The sun of God, s-u-n," Miss Harbon said thoughtfully as she pointed at the sky, "shines on our lives like the Son of God, S-o-n." Her blue eyes sparkled as she laughed.

The girls headed for their desks. It was time to begin the day.

"What is it, this about God having a son?" Rifka asked Marguerite later in the cafeteria.

"Jesus is the Son of God," Marguerite said earnestly. "He is the Saviour of the world."

Rifka frowned. "I not know that God have a son. I not understand."

Rifka's straw slurped noisily at the bottom of her glass of milk and the girls all laughed. Then, lunch was over.

School had become an enjoyable part of Rifka's life, and every weekday she eagerly went to meet her friends. "You are happy we moved to England?" her father asked her one morning as Rifka got ready to leave.

"Yes, Father," Rifka said, remembering to lower her eyes to the floor. "I like my new school. I like England."

"I wish I could say the same thing," Mamma said in a sad tone. "The weather here is so cold, and whenever I go out to the shops with Shaima, I do not understand the people. It is so difficult."

"I have heard there is an Arab market on Edgware Road. Shaima could take you there," Father said thoughtfully. He took his overcoat from a hanger and prepared to leave. "It is good we are here. Our country is becoming an increasingly recognized force in the world. *Allahu akbar.*"

Allahu akbar, Rifka thought to herself on the way to school. Allah is the greatest, her father had said. She thought back to Marguerite's statement in the cafeteria, "Jesus is the Son of God." *How is it possible for Allah to have a son? Why has no one ever told me about it?*

That afternoon in choir practice they sang the now familiar songs as well as a new one they were learning.

Jesus is the sweetest name I know,
And He's just the same, Praise His holy name.
That's the reason why I love Him so.
Jesus is the sweetest name I know!

Rifka sang the new words along with the other girls. The tune was easy for her, and by the second time they sang it, it had quickly become the favorite of many.

"I love that song!" Marguerite said after the dismissal bell rang.

"Me too," Rifka said. "The tune bounces."

As they left the school, Barbara began singing, "Jesus is the sweetest name I know . . ." and the others joined in. They walked together until one by one each of them turned off the main street to their homes.

Rifka continued on her way alone. She continued singing the new song, enjoying the tune. At first it ran along smoothly, hardly changing a note, but suddenly it rose on the scale, emphasizing "sweetest name" and gliding down on "I know." Rifka watched a pigeon sail out of the sky and land on the sidewalk, looking sideways on the bricks to find a tidbit. As Rifka approached, it rose with a whirr of wings and fled elsewhere.

Just like a bird, Rifka thought. *The song goes up and down like a flying bird.*

The next day Rifka could hardly wait for choir practice. She wanted to glide through their new song again.

The melody had been ringing in her ears all night long, and it was in her mind early in the morning when she woke up. She hummed it softly as she prepared for the day.

"You enjoy singing, don't you, Rifka?" Miss Harbon asked before choir practice that afternoon.

"Yes, ma'am," Rifka smiled at her teacher. "I enjoy much."

"That is good. Did you sing a lot in Sudan?" Miss Harbon asked as she returned the smile.

"Yes, some," Rifka replied. "In school we sing some song. At home, I sing my own song in the swing."

Miss Harbon nodded. "I can tell it is easy for you to pick up new melodies. Could you sing one of your songs for us? We would all enjoy hearing you sing a song."

"In Arabic?" Rifka laughed. "You not understand my language."

"You can tell us about the words afterward," Miss Harbon encouraged.

So, Rifka sang.

When she finished, everyone clapped. "Tell us what you sang," the girls encouraged.

"It is a song about young girl. Her mother die when she young and the girl often went out at night to see the stars. They so far away and only a little bright. The girl think of mother looking out of heaven through tiny hole in the sky that was the star. She think mother looking at her. She cry." Rifka tried to interpret the song for her classmates.

"Oh, so sad!" the girls said. "No wonder the tune is sad."

"Thank you, Rifka," Miss Harbon said. "You did a good job. God gave you a beautiful voice."

It was not the Arabic song that stayed in Rifka's mind however. It was the new chorus, "Jesus is the sweetest name I know," that kept repeating itself in her head. There was something comforting in the words. Even though Rifka could not explain what the words meant, she liked them.

The Christmas Story

CHAPTER SIX

"You are enjoying your school here in London very much, aren't you?" Rifka's father asked her one day. "You seem different than you were in Sudan."

"Oh, yes, Father, I like my school!" Rifka smiled and looked briefly into her father's eyes before dropping her gaze. "I am learning so much."

Switching to English, her father said, "And learning the English?"

Giggling, Rifka replied in English, "Yes, Papa. I learning English too."

Studying his daughter's face, Father asked, "Not

forgetting our ways, are you?"

Rifka kept her eyes on the floor and replied, "No, Papa."

November had arrived, and the school had begun preparing for their annual Christmas program. The choir from Rifka's school joined with students from other schools for this important event.

"Let's try that again," Mr. Thornton said one day, facing the choir. "The humming should be continuous, without any breaks, providing a background for the words." He looked at Rifka and with raised eyebrows asked, "Ready?"

Rifka swallowed and nodded. On cue, she began to sing:

Silent night! Holy night!
All is calm, all is bright,
Round yon virgin mother and Child;
Holy Infant, so tender and mild,
Sleep in heavenly peace,
Sleep in heavenly peace.

Her clear soprano voice soared effortlessly into the rafters of the huge church and spread out into all the corners of the cathedral.

"Excellent!" Mr. Thornton said, peering over his glasses at Rifka. "You are blessed with an amazing voice." He shook his head slightly. "So clear and pure, every note held true and steady."

Marguerite smiled at her friend with delight. Rifka smiled back self-consciously.

"So, then," Mr. Thornton turned to the choir, "let's move on to the next song."

Rifka slipped back into the choir and prepared herself for the next selection.

When December arrived, the practice sessions became more frequent.

"There are usually over two thousand people present on Christmas evening," Marguerite told Rifka. "You will be singing in front of many people. Aren't you excited?"

Rifka nodded. "And nervous," she admitted. Turning to her friend, she said, "I have question. What is important about Christmas? What does this person Jesus have to do with us? This is new. I not understand."

The two girls were on the sidewalk, walking home from school. They ignored the gray skies and cold wind as they walked along chatting, burrowed deep inside their warm coats.

"I have heard the story about Christmas ever since I was small," Marguerite said with a tiny frown. "I have always believed it, and it never occurred to me that other people wouldn't know about it."

The two walked on in silence. Then Marguerite spoke. "I have an idea, Rifka. Come home with me, and I will ask my mother to explain it to you. Okay?"

Rifka had been to Marguerite's house before, so she readily agreed.

"Mamma, can you tell Rifka the Christmas story?" Marguerite asked when they entered her apartment. "Like you do for us on Christmas Day?"

"Certainly!" Mrs. Roberts replied. "Come, sit down here beside the heater."

Beginning with the angel's appearance to Mary, Mrs. Roberts told Rifka the story. In detail she told the little Sudanese girl about the journey Joseph and Mary made toward Bethlehem and how there was no place for them to stay when they arrived. She told how Jesus had been born in a cattle shelter. She described the appearance of the angels to the shepherds and the shepherds' response to the good news. Vividly she told of the wise men's trip to find the infant King.

"That is beautiful story," said Rifka. "But if Jesus was with God in heaven, why He came here to be baby? And what does this story have for people today?"

"Those are very good questions, Rifka," Mrs. Roberts said. "Jesus came to earth because of love. It would have been much easier for Him to stay in heaven, but because He loved people so much, He came to earth. You will hear more of this story later, but when Jesus became older, He died and became a sacrifice for all people. He did this so that everyone who believes on Him can live in heaven forever. That is why we celebrate Christmas every year," Mrs. Roberts finished.

"Thank you very much," Rifka said, her mind trying to fit this story into the words of the songs they had been practicing. "I must go now so Mamma is not worried."

That evening Rifka lay in bed, her mind busy with the amazing story she had heard. *Amazing that a tiny baby, born to a young girl, could be the Son of God! Why did God need a Son? Was one God not enough? Amazing that Jesus would leave heaven to come to earth and be born in a barn just because He loved people so much.* Rifka could not make sense of it all, but for some reason she couldn't stop thinking about it.

"Silent night! Holy night! All is calm, all is bright . . ." she sang, loving the way the tune wrapped itself around the words and cradled them with sound.

In the next verse, Rifka came to the stirring words, "Glories stream from heaven afar, Heavenly hosts sing alleluia! Christ the Saviour is born! Christ the Saviour is born." Forgetting that she was supposed to be sleeping, she let her voice sing out with gladness, just the way Mr. Thornton had told her to do.

As she sang, her mind was busy picturing the shepherds outside tending their sheep, just the way the shepherds back in Sudan tended their flocks. She had often seen them when she had traveled in her father's car to another city. It was easy to imagine the surprise and shock with which the shepherds long ago had looked up to see the angel coming. How astonished they must have been to hear that a King had been born close by in a town called Bethlehem!

"Rifka!" There was a knock on the door, and she heard her father's voice from the hall outside. The door opened, and she could see her father's figure outlined by the hall light as he stood in the doorway.

Rifka sat up in bed. Her father never came to her room, never knocked on her door, and never called her name like that! What was happening?

"Rifka, what are you singing?" Her father spoke in Arabic, his tone harsh.

"A song," Rifka said, her voice trembling. "A song I learned at school. For the program."

Father's breath exploded loudly, and he said, "A Christian song!"

"I don't know, Father," Rifka said honestly. "It is a song for Christmas."

"We are Muslims!" Father said loudly. "We don't have Christmas. I sent you to school to learn English, not to learn about a foreign religion! We are Muslims and Mohammad is our prophet! *Allahu akbar!*" He threw the words challengingly into the room.

"*Allahu akbar,*" Rifka said quickly. "Yes, Father!"

"This will stop," Father said with authority. "You will not be singing songs about Christmas! I will speak with the teachers tomorrow!"

At first Rifka made no answer. Then the enormity of her father's words began to sink in. "But, I am a soloist!" The words came unbidden. "I sing the opening song!"

"Quiet! You have no say in this matter!" Father spoke loudly. "You have been taught to obey! You are a Muslim, not a Christian. Do you understand?"

Rifka nodded and said obediently, "Yes, Father." She did not know what "Christian" really meant. But it must not be acceptable to Muslims.

The door closed with a bang, and Rifka could hear Father talking loudly to Mamma. Even though the door was closed, she could hear many of his words. With a trembling heart she heard him say, ". . . might have to take Rifka out of school."

Not go to school? That would be worse than not singing in choir anymore! What would she do? Where would she go to school?

Rifka lay shivering under her covers, her nerves tense

and her mind going in circles. What was going to happen? Would she be able to go to school tomorrow? Who would sing her song? The program was less than two weeks away.

"All is calm, all is bright!" The words of her song came to her gently and soothingly as the unanswered questions ran through her mind. "Christ the Saviour is born!"

Fragments of song seemingly came out of the night and found a resting place in her head. She thought of another song they sang in the program and how the opening words rang out suddenly, "Joy to the world, the Lord is come! Let earth receive her King!"

She thought back to her life in Sudan. There, no one had ever told her about Jesus. No one had told her the story of the shepherds and the wise men, the story about Mary and Joseph and the baby King.

Rifka remembered her prayers with her mother. They still said their Muslim prayers in London. Whenever she was at home for prayer time, she knelt to pray. She knew her father went to a mosque in London every Friday to say his prayers. He often complained about how far he had to travel on the bus to get there. But as a good

Muslim, he always went.

Was everyone's god the same? Was the god that her parents prayed to the same God who had a son? A son named Jesus? It was all so confusing to Rifka.

Again, snatches of school songs came into Rifka's mind. She did not dare sing them aloud. But they would not stay away.

"Silent night! Holy night! . . . love's pure Light! Radiant beams from thy holy face . . . Jesus, Lord, at thy birth." Those words were talking straight to Jesus! About His birth! How was it possible to talk to Jesus?

Something inside her told her to try. Rifka did. "Jesus, can you hear me? Can you hear me, a girl from Sudan?"

Every day in school Rifka had heard the teachers lead in prayer. It was a part of school. She knew Marguerite prayed with her parents. Many of the pupils prayed.

But would Jesus hear the prayer of a Muslim girl from Sudan who had never heard of Him before she came to England? Rifka wasn't sure.

"Jesus, if you do hear and care for me, thank you." Her first prayer was hesitant and questioning, but it was prayed in sincerity.

That night in her dreams, Rifka kept hearing her father's voice telling her in Arabic that she was a Muslim. But all during the dream, louder than her father's words, came the words from her song:

Silent night! Holy night!
All is calm, all is bright,
Round yon virgin mother and Child;
Holy Infant, so tender and mild,
Sleep in heavenly peace,
Sleep in heavenly peace.

"You May Not Sing!"

CHAPTER SEVEN

Rifka felt the eyes of her classmates as she walked alongside her father into the school building the next day. Even Marguerite asked questions with her eyes, but Rifka said nothing. In fact, most of the time she looked down at the brown squares of the tiles during the long walk to the principal's office.

"My daughter will not sing in that, that Christmas thing," Father said loudly and sternly as he faced the surprised Mrs. Smelcher in her office. "We are Muslims. We do not believe your holidays. We do not have Christmas."

"Why, sir," Mrs. Smelcher said with a smile, "you must

come sometime and listen to them when they practice. Your daughter has a beautiful voice. I always try to make sure I am somewhere close to the choir when they practice because I love to hear her sing."

At this unexpected praise of his daughter, Father looked quickly at Rifka, but she did not meet his gaze. She was still looking down at the floor. He addressed Mrs. Smelcher again, but his voice was less stern. "But it is not in our religion. We are Muslims. *Allahu akbar!*"

"We try to respect all people from every nation and religion," Mrs. Smelcher said. "We have students from different nationalities here, as you know, and we welcome them all. However, we are a Christian school and we do celebrate Christian holidays. We do not force our beliefs onto anyone who attends, but we value our loyalty to God and to Jesus Christ. I firmly believe this is what makes our school a noted school of excellence, sir. As you already know, our students consistently grade among the highest in London."

Rifka waited silently as the dialogue continued between her father and Mrs. Smelcher. She felt relief trickling through her as she heard her father's voice settle into the familiar respectful tone he used when speaking with foreigners.

"I coming today to hear Rifka sing," he said after a period of silence. "It is at two and a half o'clock?"

All during her regular classes, Rifka both dreaded and anticipated the choir practice. At times she felt a glow of happiness that her father actually showed enough interest to come and listen to her sing. Other times she cringed as she thought of his strong words against her singing Christian songs.

In her history class she let her mind drift away from what the teacher was saying. *What is a Christian? Why does it matter so much to Father if I believe the story of Jesus? How is my life different from the English children? Does it matter what or in whom people believe?*

"I'm not really hungry," she explained to Marguerite at lunchtime, "even though I do really like this . . . this cottage pie." She looked at the juices oozing from a crack in the hot pastry on her plate.

"Worried about this afternoon?" Marguerite asked. "Must be hard not to know what your father will say."

Rifka felt tears sting her eyelids, and she could not

answer. Marguerite squeezed her hand sympathetically, and Rifka managed a weak smile.

That afternoon when they filed into the cathedral to begin their practice session, she looked into the vast space where the pews stretched toward the entry. Her heart lurched when she saw, not only her father, but also her mother sitting close to the front, right next to the center aisle!

The director lifted his hand, and the students hummed the first lines of "Silent Night." At the cue from the director, Rifka began singing.

Silent night! Holy night!
All is calm, all is bright,
Round yon virgin mother and Child;
Holy Infant, so tender and mild,
Sleep in heavenly peace,
Sleep in heavenly peace.

Rifka's clear voice faltered only a little at the beginning, and then it swelled among the lofty rafters of the church. Her eyes caught the stained glass window that showed the infant Jesus in a stable and Mary and Jo-

seph bending over Him. Fixing her gaze on it, she sang the familiar lines.

The choir echoed the last two lines of the song, and Rifka began the next verse.

Silent night! Holy night!
Shepherds quake at the sight!
Glories stream from heaven afar,
Heavenly hosts sing alleluia!
Christ the Saviour is born!
Christ the Saviour is born.

As the choir hummed the tune and joined Rifka in singing the glad news, "Christ the Saviour is born!" the entire cathedral rang with their glad voices.

Rifka closed her eyes as she began the last verse.

Silent night! Holy night!
Son of God, love's pure Light,
Radiant beams from thy holy face,
With the dawn of redeeming grace,
Jesus, Lord, at thy birth!
Jesus, Lord, at thy birth.

Rifka held the last note and different voices from the choir echoed the last line until the entire choir was weaving the glorious lines of the last verse in and out of her note, rising and falling into a beautiful tapestry of sound.

As silence fell and before they could begin the next song, Rifka watched her father stand up and pull Mamma up beside him. Stepping into the aisle, he walked forward purposefully and said loudly, “Rifka, come!”

It did not occur to Rifka not to obey. She had been taught instant obedience to her father for as long as she could remember. But inside, she felt shame and humiliation as she stepped out of her place and walked toward her parents.

Mercifully, the choir director began the next song and the dreadful silence ended before they walked out the front doors, but Rifka felt as though she could not get outside quickly enough.

There were no words spoken as the three walked down the steps, up the short distance on the sidewalk to the school, and once more down the hall to Mrs. Smelcher’s office.

When Father knocked on the closed door, there was no response from inside, but behind them they heard her voice. "I'm coming," she said pleasantly, and it was comforting to Rifka to hear the familiar voice of the school director.

"Rifka will not sing in the program. She will not sing Christian songs. She is a Muslim and she must stay a Muslim." Father did not speak in a loud, angry voice, but his words were firm. "I do not want my daughter to change religion."

"I had hoped that when you heard your daughter sing, you would change your mind, sir," Mrs. Smelcher said. Rifka could tell from her tone of voice that Mrs. Smelcher really was sad about the decision her father had made. "Nevertheless, we will respect your wishes."

Father leaned forward. "I do not want Rifka to help with any Christian singing. I understand you have daily—what do you call it, chapel? I want her excused."

Mrs. Smelcher looked at the three people in her office and briefly closed her eyes. Lifting her gaze, she said, "That, I cannot agree to. We have a school policy that all students must adhere to the curriculum we have chosen, and the daily chapel is a part of that curriculum. Although we would not want to have Rifka leave our school, you do have the choice to withdraw her from here and enroll her in the school of your choice."

Rifka could hear the clock on the wall tick loudly as Mrs. Smelcher's words hung in the air. She found it difficult to breathe.

"I will let you know my decision," Father finally said. "You will have your answer tomorrow morning. Come, Rifka."

Nothing was said about the matter on the walk home. They walked through the busy London streets without a word. When they reached their apartment, Rifka took her homework into her room. After she closed the door, she could hear her parents' voices in their bedroom.

Rifka sat at the small table she used for a desk and tried to complete her arithmetic assignment. But the problems did not seem to make any sense, and she found herself adding when she should have subtracted.

What kind of school would Father enroll me in if he does decide I may no longer attend this school? She knew there were plenty of other schools, even close by, for she often saw other students in their own particular uniforms on the streets.

Her mind drifted back to her first days of school, and she vividly remembered how awkward she had felt. *Will I have to make new friends all over again? What if no one likes me at the new school?*

Rifka ate her dinner with her parents, and no one talked about Rifka's schooling. But before she left the table to finish her homework, Father suddenly said, "Rifka, bring me your school reports."

Rifka went to her room and found the brown envelope that held the six-week reports from each of her classes. She handed the envelope to her father. Without a word he took it and put it on the table beside his plate. With a nod, he dismissed his daughter.

Rifka Sings!
CHAPTER EIGHT

"Rifka, you will not sing."

Father repeated his decision from the day before at the breakfast table the next morning.

Rifka had just taken a bite of toast as he spoke, and for a moment she thought she would choke. She quickly took a drink of milk from her cup and placed it carefully on the tabletop.

"We are Muslims, *Allahu akbar*," Father continued, "and we will not have our daughter singing Christian songs."

Rifka held her breath. Would she also be removed from school and sent to another one?

"You will continue to attend classes there," Father continued, facing Rifka. "The education system is the best we can get for you close by, and your grades reflect the excellence of the teaching program."

Rifka's chest heaved as she let her breath out slowly and a flood of joy swept over her. She could still attend her beloved school! She wanted to shout and sing, but that would not be acceptable to her parents, so she sat quietly in a pool of happiness.

"I can never sing 'Silent Night' like you do," Marguerite told Rifka sadly in school that day. "I am so sorry you can't do the solo!"

Rifka smiled. "It is okay," she said bravely. "I am not allowed to sing in the program, but oh, Marguerite, I don't have to change schools! That makes me so happy!"

Even though her heart ached all during choir practice as she sat in the library, blindly paging through books, she kept reminding herself, "At least I can continue coming to this school." Then an amazing thing happened. She heard her own voice whisper, "Thank you, Jesus!"

It caught her by surprise. Where had those words come from? She remembered hearing Miss Harbon say it, and once Marguerite had hugged her test results and said, “Thank you, Jesus.” But Rifka had never said that. She was a Muslim.

It was on the day of the program that Shaima told Mamma, “This evening I want to take Rifka to buy the special candy that is available only at Christmas. I will take good care of her.”

Rifka enjoyed the evening with Shaima. The city was full of shoppers and the atmosphere was festive. And, as they were walking home, they approached the cathedral where Rifka had spent so many hours practicing.

As they got closer, Rifka could see that the doors of the cathedral were open wide to welcome any latecomers. She hurried closer and peeked inside. “Let's stay and listen!” she begged Shaima. Shaima said nothing, but halted and peered in the doors with Rifka.

Inside, the huge cathedral was almost full. Hundreds of people crowded the pews to hear the wonderful story of Christ's birth through songs. No matter that most of the people had heard the story all of their lives. No matter that every year many of the same carols were sung. It was Christmas, a time to remember and celebrate. Jesus Christ, the Saviour for all men, had come into the world as a tiny baby. The words of "Silent Night" floated out into the frosty night air.

Rifka shivered and snuggled deeper into her winter coat. It was strange, being outside the cathedral, looking in the open door and seeing the choir standing in the front. Without her. She felt for a minute as though she were two people, one standing here in the cold, and one in front of the crowd, singing with the group of students with whom she had spent so much time preparing for the Christmas program.

Rifka heard the choir voices die down in preparation for the second verse of "Silent Night." She remembered how the director always looked down at his shoes, until just at the right moment, when the new verse was to start, he would raise both eyebrows high on his forehead.

The words of the second verse swelled up inside the huge cathedral and filled the air with beauty. In waves, the music washed out through the open door. Rifka could not help herself. She began to sing from her hiding place, "Silent night! Holy night! Shepherds quake at the sight . . ."

Anyone on the sidewalks might have been taken by surprise as a small girl standing in front of the giant cathedral doors echoed the music coming from the cathedral. Cars and buses buzzed past, but Rifka didn't pay attention. She let her voice rise as the words from the song echoed in her ears. All the way to the end of the song, she sang.

When the last note of "Silent Night" had ended, Shaima said, "Come!" and Rifka reluctantly pulled herself away from the church doors. Slowly she followed Shaima down the street to their house.

All the way home the words of the song floated through Rifka's head. She laughed as she thought about how surprised Marguerite would be if she knew that she, Rifka, had been singing along with her.

Back home in her bed that night, Rifka hugged her arms tightly across her chest and buried herself in her thoughts. So she had sung in the program after all,

though no one inside the cathedral had heard her. Was it because Jesus really had heard her when she talked to Him? Had He known how much she wanted to sing, and given her the chance?

"Silent night! Holy night!" The words of her song kept echoing inside Rifka's mind as she lay in her bed. Even though she did not dare sing loudly, her voice rose and fell in whispers as she continued the song until the end.

Suddenly it seemed as though she were no longer in her bed. It was as if she had been somehow transported into a land much more similar to Sudan than England. She was hurrying down a rough stone road in the dark with a group of people, all of them going toward a stable on the outskirts of a village. Rifka strained her eyes, and in the distance it seemed she could see a light shining brightly in the stable. As they came closer, she could see a woman and man looking down into a feed box. There in that box was a baby.

Rifka felt herself kneeling with the crowd. Some shepherds were there as well as townspeople. But no one was looking at each other. They were all gazing at the baby lying on some straw in the feed box.

"Jesus, Lord, at thy birth!" Rifka sang out, her voice ringing in the night air. And all around her, other voices took up the song until the skies echoed with the triumphant words, "Christ the Saviour is born!"

About the Author

Harvey Yoder and his wife Karen live in the beautiful mountains of western North Carolina. They have five children, all of whom are married, and nine grandchildren. A teacher for many years, Harvey is now a licensed real estate agent in addition to being a prolific writer. He has traveled extensively while gathering materials for his many books, most of which have been published by Christian Aid Ministries. Harvey finds it especially fulfilling to write the inspiring accounts of faithful believers whose stories would otherwise remain unknown. His greatest desire in writing is that his readers will not merely be entertained by the stories, but rather be motivated to seek God with all their hearts.

Harvey enjoys hearing from readers and can be contacted by e-mail at harveYoder@juno.com or written in care of Christian Aid Ministries, P.O. Box 360, Berlin, Ohio, 44610.

Additional Books
BY HARVEY YODER

God Knows My Size!
How God answered Silvia Tarniceriu's specific prayer

251 pages $10.99

They Would Not Be Silent
Testimonies of persecuted Christians in Eastern Europe

231 pages $10.99

They Would Not Be Moved
More testimonies of Christians who stood strong under communism

208 pages $10.99

Elena—Strengthened Through Trials
A young Romanian girl strengthened through hardships

240 pages $10.99

Where Little Ones Cry
The sad trails of abandoned children in Liberia during civil war

168 pages plus 16-page picture section $10.99

Wang Ping's Sacrifice
Vividly portrays the house church in China

191 pages $10.99

A Small Price to Pay
Mikhail Khorev's story of suffering under communism

247 pages $10.99

Tsunami!—from a few that survived
Survivors tell their stories, some with sorrow and heartbreak, others with joy and hope.

168 pages $11.99

A Greater Call
What will it cost Wei to spread the Gospel in China?

195 pages $11.99

The Happening
Nickel Mines school shooting—healing and forgiveness

173 pages $11.99

In Search of Home
The true story of a Muslim family's miraculous conversion

240 pages $11.99

Miss Nancy
The fascinating story of God's work through the life of an Amish missionary in Belize

273 pages $11.99

Into Their Hands
Bible smugglers find ingenious ways to transport Bibles into Romania and the former Soviet Union.

194 pages $11.99

A Life Redeemed
The inspiring story of Ludlow Walker's journey from his childhood in Jamaica to his current calling as a minister of the Gospel. An unforgettable story of God's redeeming grace and transforming power.

232 pages $11.99

Bread for the Winter
Eight-year-old Pavel learns from his godly parents what Jesus meant when He said, "Love your enemies . . ."

72 pages $4.99

Vera, the King's Daughter
The story of this unlikely princess, set in the plains of central Ukraine, will inspire all who meet her through the pages of this book.

208 pages $11.99

A Good Different
Only a miracle could restore the shattered lives of this Kenyan couple. Their story will cause you to marvel anew at how God heals the brokenhearted and gives beauty for ashes.

255 pages $12.99